PHOENIX

Mark Dawson

AN UNPUTDOWNABLE book.

First published in Great Britain in 2017 by
UNPUTDOWNABLE LIMITED

Copyright © UNPUTDOWNABLE LIMITED 2017

Formatting by Polgarus Studio

The moral right of Mark Dawson to be identified as the author of this work has been asserted by him in accordance with the Copyright, Designs and Patents Act 1988.

All the characters in this book are fictitious, and any resemblance to actual persons living or dead is purely coincidental.

All rights reserved. No part of this publication may be reproduced, stored in a retrieval system or transmitted in any form or by any means, without the prior permission in writing of the publisher, nor to be otherwise circulated in any form of binding or cover other than that in which it is published without a similar condition, including this condition, being imposed on the subsequent purchaser.

For Emma, Matt and Phoenix.

Part One

Chapter One

Beatrix Rose waited in the antechamber outside the office. She *hated* to wait. Punctuality was important, and it had been drilled into her during her time in the military. Control had asked to see her at midday, and she had been here on time. It was twenty past now, and she knew that either he didn't care what she thought of being made to wait or he was making a point. It was, she suspected, the latter. Control was not the sort of man to do anything without consideration, and she guessed that he was reminding her who was in command of Group Fifteen. She was Number One, the senior agent, but it was Control who sent her, and the fourteen others with whom she worked, out on assignment. There had been one conversation that she recalled, near the start of her career in the Group, when he had suggested that he was a craftsman and that the fifteen of them were his tools. She had taken an instant dislike to him then, and nothing that had happened in the intervening period had changed her mind.

Captain Tanner guarded access to the door. He was Control's private secretary and managed the inconveniences of his position with a warm smile and ready wit that belied the fact that, by rights, he should have been resentful. His leg had been blown off by an IED on the road outside Kabul. A promising career had been forestalled and replaced with a life as a superannuated functionary, making excuses for his boss when he pulled rude stunts like this.

There was a light above the door that shone red when Control was not to be disturbed. Beatrix remembered a doctor she had seen when she had been a child; there had been a similar system then, but that was thirty years ago.

"Ah," Tanner said, looking up at the light. It had changed to green. "He'll see you now, Number One. Sorry for the wait. Please—go through."

#

The office was large and pleasant. Beatrix was not in the habit of frequenting the members' clubs that could be found off Pall Mall, but she imagined that those rooms would have more in common with this office than the offices of similarly senior intelligence officers in the SIS building at Vauxhall Cross. There was a wide window that offered a view out onto the Thames, and the prints on the walls had been expensively framed. There was a fireplace with a marble mantelpiece, and sitting atop it were pictures of Control's wife and three children and another of him as a much younger man wearing full military uniform.

Control was seated behind his enormous desk. There was no computer; he was too old-fashioned to use one and still dictated his communiqués for the secretaries in the typing pool that Beatrix guessed was maintained solely for his benefit. His emails were delivered to him in a leather folder for him to scribble his amendments in red ink.

He looked up as Beatrix approached the desk. "Sit

"What do you want me to do?"

"The CIA wants him back. They don't have an active network in Caracas and we do, so we're doing them a favour, as I said. Returning him is the primary goal. But, between us, we'd like to know why he's got them so worked up. So your orders are these: find him, secure him, then question him." He let that word—*question*—hang in the air, although it really wasn't necessary, because Beatrix knew exactly what it encompassed.

"What do we want to know?"

"Read the file. The short version is this: the working assumption is that he left Daedalus because someone was offering to pay him a lot of money. It's likely another country—the Chinese, most likely, but maybe the French or the Germans. It could even be the Russians trying to take him back again. We'd like to know who it was, the circumstances behind his decision, and the agents who recruited him. But more important than that is what he's been doing. Langley won't tell us and, frankly, we'd like a briefing. It's the least we deserve after helping them out."

"And then?"

"Exfiltrate him. The Navy has a frigate in the region to stop the local smugglers. They'll send a boat to pick you up."

"Yes, sir."

"The usual protocols apply to this, Number One. You're deniable, so don't get caught."

"Do I have any backup?"

"You do. There's a man waiting for you. He's SAS."

She scanned the file without finding mention of him. "The name?"

"Major John Milton."

She shook her head. "Never heard of him."

"He's been on our radar for a while, as it happens. Comes highly recommended. You've got a meet set up with him in Caracas tomorrow. Travel has sorted out your flight and accommodation. You leave tonight."

"Yes, sir." She got up, collected the file and turned for the door.

Control stood, too. "One other thing, Beatrix."

"Yes, sir?"

"And this is probably nothing. I'm almost loath to bring it up."

"Sir?"

He winced, as if the subject he wanted to bring up was distasteful to him. "Are you—well, are you all *right*, Number One?"

"Of course," Beatrix replied. "Why do you say that?"

"Your annual evaluation. I've looked it over. It's fine—everything's where I'd expect it to be, and your work has been excellent, as usual. But they're still recommending referral."

"Why would they say that?"

"They think you're showing signs of distraction. Is that true, Beatrix? Are you distracted?"

She shook her head and, careful not to stare him down, held his gaze. "No, sir," she said, with as much calm sincerity as she could find. "I'm not. Nothing's changed."

"You're still committed to our work? It's not—"

"Completely," she said, talking over him. "I'm as committed as when you recruited me. More, in fact. I've seen the world now. What it's like. What happens in the dark corners. What our enemies are prepared to do. I know better than ever that what we do is important. You don't need to worry, sir. They can refer me if they like. But they'll send me back clean."

Control smiled; as ever, Beatrix found his off-white, vulpine teeth unpleasant. "I don't think that'll be necessary," he said. "Knew it was nothing. Good luck, Number One. Enjoy the sun."

Chapter Two

Beatrix hurried to make her appointment. The clinic was on Harley Street in Marylebone. She took a taxi from Vauxhall Cross and, thanks to traffic as they passed Buckingham Palace, she was five minutes late. Her husband, Lucas, was in the waiting room.

"Sorry," she said. "Traffic."

"It's fine." He smiled as he kissed her.

Beatrix found that she was anxious, an uncomfortable ache in her stomach. Lucas was nervous, too; he told her as much when she left the house this morning, but he hid it beneath another warm smile as they sat down next to one another. He took her hand in his and squeezed it.

"Are you okay?" he asked.

"Yes," she said. "Just... well, you know."

"Don't worry. We need to know. Whatever it is, we'll adjust."

The receptionist looked at her screen and then looked up at them. "Dr. Wells is ready," she said. "You can go through."

#

Dr. Wells was a middle-aged man with a warm smile and a comforting attitude. He was expensive, but Beatrix and Lucas had decided that they would not allow budgetary concerns to prevent them from engaging the best professional available. And one thing down, Number One," he said, flicking his fingers in the direction of one of the chairs. It was a repulsive gesture, at once dismissive and demeaning, as if he were shaking something distasteful from his manicured nails.

She did as she was told, waiting quietly as he finished amending the document he had been working on. He sighed, swore under his breath, and pushed the piece of paper away.

"You wanted to see me, sir?" Beatrix said.

"Yes, I do. I have something for you."

Control picked up a file and slid it across the desk. The Group had been active for many years and still maintained some of the same protocols that it had adopted in its early years. Some of those continued methods were because of administrative inertia, but others had become more useful as technology had ostensibly left them behind. The Group's files were a case in point. Mission orders were typed on paper and provided to the receiving agent within a manila folder. It was a curious anachronism, but justified because these files—proof that Her Majesty's agencies occasionally reached out from Vauxhall Cross and snuffed out lives around the world—would have been politically incendiary if a hacker had been able to break the security on the SIS servers.

Beatrix opened the file and flicked through the meagre papers.

"I can give you the summary," Control said. "The target's name is Igor Koralev. He's a geneticist, Russian by birth. Seventy-four years old, although he's fit and active for his age. He emigrated to the USA just after the collapse of the Soviet Union and has lived just outside Boston ever since. He's a widower. He's rich, no wife or any other family that we've been able to ascertain. He's cautious and careful and very smart. He might be old, but this won't be easy."

"Genetics?"

"That's right," Control said. "But it doesn't matter what he does. He's a job. No more, no less."

"So why are we after him?"

"We're doing a favour for the Americans. Koralev and a colleague worked for the Soviets. This was twenty years ago—a classified program, some kind of research. Genetics, as I say. From what we know, they saw how much money they stood to make in the real world and they defected. They offered their work to the CIA, Langley said yes, and they continued to work on it in a multimillion-dollar facility just outside Boston. The CIA set them up with a front company and poured money into the project."

Beatrix read down the first page of the briefing. "This is Daedalus Genetics?"

"That's right. They've been engaged in R&D, for the most part, taking money out of the DARPA budget. But it turns out that Igor is even more greedy than the Russians or the Americans expected. He and his colleague were due to attend a meeting at Langley last month, but he never showed up. The CIA asked us for help and GCHQ found him when he turned up in Caracas. That's where he is now—Venezuela. You've got pictures in the file that a local stringer shot of him last week."

was clear: Dr. Wells was an authority on his subject. Their previous appointments with him had been productive, and they both had confidence that he would provide them with the information—and, if necessary, the treatment—that they needed.

They sat down opposite him in his well-appointed office. An assistant brought in a tray of coffee and biscuits.

Beatrix shifted uncomfortably, anxious to get started. "Do you have the results?" she asked.

"I do," the doctor said. He gave her a consoling smile, and Beatrix felt her stomach plunge. "I'm afraid the news isn't what we might have hoped."

Lucas squeezed Beatrix's hand. "Go on," he said.

"As you know, we tested you both. I'll start with you, Beatrix."

She thought that she was going to be sick.

"The ultrasound showed no obvious issues. Your egg reserve is fine. Your biological clock has years left to run. Your ovaries are in good shape, certainly healthy enough to ripen eggs. The blood flow to your ovaries and follicles was checked with what we call a colour and power Doppler and, again, it was excellent. We assessed your uterus: no polyps, fibroids or any other factors affecting implantation or anything that might cause miscarriage. And the blood flow to the uterus and the lining of your womb was also good. There is no reason why you wouldn't be able to implant embryos, and your chances of miscarriage are the same as any other fit and healthy woman of your age." He shrugged, as if dismissing any concerns that he might have had regarding her. "There's nothing wrong with you at all, Beatrix. You should be able to conceive."

"So it's me?" Lucas said. "I'm the problem?"

Wells looked at him sympathetically. "Well," he said, "it does appear that that's where the problem is arising."

"Or not," Lucas said, his joke falling flat. Beatrix squeezed his hand; he relied on humour when he felt vulnerable, and she knew that he felt exposed now.

"We ran the full battery of tests, Lucas. And it seems that you were dealt a bad hand when you were born. Fertility is often a matter of genetics, and there's not much that can be done if you are unfortunate in that regard. We think you have what's known as Klinefelter syndrome. It's a chromosomal condition that affects male physical and cognitive development. It's caused by a subject having one additional X chromosome. It interferes with male sexual development, often preventing the testes from functioning normally and reducing the levels of testosterone."

"Is it something I got from my parents?"

"No. You can't inherit it. Research suggests it's caused by random events when the eggs and sperm are forming in the parents."

"Can it be treated?" he asked.

"There are options," Wells said. "We can look at collecting your sperm. We would obtain a sample using a thin needle inserted into the testicle or through a small incision made in the testicle. Normal sperm are identified and then used for in vitro fertilisation."

"What are the chances of success?"

"Honestly? Not amazing. Twenty or thirty per cent."

Lucas nodded. "And how much does it cost?"

"I'll have to put together a quote. But it's not cheap. The extraction and a round of IVF would probably be in the twenty-thousand-pound range. We are on the higher end of the scale here, of course. You might be able to get a clinic to do it for fifteen, perhaps."

Beatrix felt dizzy. They didn't have that kind of money. She stood, Lucas's hand slipping from her fingers. "Thank you, Doctor," she said.

"Would you like me to quote?"

Her thoughts were muddied. She shook her head, mumbled her thanks, and opened the door to the main reception area. Lucas stood, thanked the doctor, and hurried after her. She collected her coat and started for the door, ignoring the cheery farewell from the receptionist. Lucas caught up with her as she descended the stairs, pushed open the door and stepped out into the crisp afternoon.

He put his hand on her shoulder. "Hey," he said. "It's okay. We'll find a way."

"How?" she said. "We don't have that kind of money."

"We just need to think about it. We could get a loan. I could speak to my parents."

"No," she said. She felt a hotness on her cheeks, and her eyes started to well with tears. She blinked furiously, fighting to maintain her composure. She hated to show weakness, even in front of her husband.

Yet as she stood there, the world carrying on around them, the traffic passing along the grand buildings that smelt of money and privilege, clinics that represented hope and opportunity that she knew they would never be able to afford, she didn't resist Lucas as he brought her into an embrace and held her tight.

Parque Nacional Laguna de la Restinga, the fifty sandy beaches, the fabulous surf off the Playa El Yaque and the boat trips into the mangrove, where pelicans and flamingos could be observed.

By the time Beatrix was au fait with the detail, she was tempted to return with Lucas so that they could enjoy the facilities for themselves. She knew, of course, that that would not be possible. For one, they wouldn't be able to afford it. And the meetings would not go ahead—an excuse had been prepared—and ops would handle the follow-up correspondence. Boutique Getaways was a real company, with a website and real customers who had no idea that their patronage was contributing to a front that allowed Group Fifteen agents to move about the world under a cloak of fake legitimacy. It was likely that Margarita Island would feature among the company's future destinations. The deception was thorough and utterly credible. No expense was spared in making it so; no inconvenience was enough to prompt an easier path.

Next, Beatrix read the details of the man she had been sent to retrieve. There was nothing on the work that Koralev and his colleague had been doing at Daedalus. It didn't concern Beatrix. She didn't need to know the background, and, in some ways, it was better that she didn't know. There was always the chance that she might be detained during her mission and, in the event that she was questioned, what she did not know could not be revealed. Her training had included hours of simulated torture that brushed up close to the real thing, and she was as prepared for that eventuality as

Chapter Three

Beatrix flew Air France to Caracas, changing at Charles de Gaulle. The Group's Op Support desk had put together a comprehensive legend so that she could go about her business in Venezuela without drawing undue attention to herself or to the true reason for her visit. She had transferred the details to her laptop and settled safely in business class with no possibility that she could be overlooked by her fellow passengers, she opened the files. She was fastidious about preparation, and, even though she had already absorbed the information, she decided to review it all again. And, more than her desire to be prepared, throwing herself into her work would be a distraction from the riot of thoughts that she had struggled to contain since the meeting at the clinic that afternoon.

And so she read. Her name was Rebecca Smith. She was married to John Smith, and the two of them—husband and wife—were the proprietors of Boutique Getaways, a travel agency that specialised in providing well-heeled travellers with expensive holidays to unusual parts of the world. Meetings had been arranged for the Smiths with hoteliers on the Isla de Margarita, a destination in the Caribbean about forty kilometres to the north of the mainland. There was a page of notes extolling the virtues of the island, and Beatrix spent time memorising them: the two peninsulas linked by sand and the mangroves of the she could possibly be. But that would not insulate her from all eventualities. An interrogator armed with sodium thiopental, for example, could remove her inhibitions and loosen the firm knots that her training allowed her to tie; it would be useless, though, in extracting information that she did not know.

She moved on to the asset who was waiting to assist her. John Milton was an orphan whose parents had been killed in a car crash on the German Autobahn when he was twelve. Upon their deaths, the inheritance Milton received paid for a first-class education that had taken him to Cambridge. He had turned down the offer of a pupillage at the Bar to enlist with the Royal Green Jackets. He had been posted to Winchester and then sent to Gibraltar. He had served in Northern Ireland and was, according to his superior officers, an excellent soldier. He had been persuaded to apply for Selection to the SAS and passed with ease. His career with Air Troop, B Squadron, 22 SAS had been spectacular: he had served in the Middle East, the Far East, South and Central America and had then gone back to Armagh. Milton had notched up multiple kills and had been pegged as a particularly dogged operator; indeed, his name had been added to a list of potential recruits to Group Fifteen. As Number One, Beatrix could remove him from that list as quickly as clicking her fingers. But there were no blemishes on his record. Beatrix could see why he had been chosen.

She deleted the files, wiping her hard drive of them completely, and then opened her email client. She hovered the cursor over one unread email, wanting to open it yet reluctant to do so. The email had been sent from Action for Children, an adoption agency in South London. Beatrix had filled out a form on their website and sent it off while she waited at the airport, requesting information on the services that they provided. They had responded at once, within an hour of the form being completed, but, although she had looked at it several times, sitting in her inbox, Beatrix had been unable to open it. She knew why: it was an admission of failure, acceptance of the fact that she and Lucas would not be able to conceive a child themselves. It was second best. She wasn't ready to consider that.

She closed the laptop, slid it into her bag and stowed it in her overhead locker. The flight from Paris to Caracas was ten hours. She reclined her seat, put a sleeping mask over her face and closed her eyes.

Control had been right: she *was* distracted. Sleep would help.

Chapter Four

One of the benefits of a legend that painted her as a high-end travel agent was that Beatrix was accommodated in some of the best hotels in the world. Ops had booked Rebecca Smith a suite at the Cayena Hotel, a five-star establishment that was reputed to be the best in Caracas. A limousine had been sent to meet her at the airport and the polite and discreet driver had delivered her to the Avenida Principal La Castellana. The hotel was housed within a sleek building that was at odds with the poorer areas that they had passed through on the hour-long drive through Maiquetía and then the fringes of the city.

A bellhop opened the door of the car and welcomed her to the hotel. She stepped out, exchanging the pleasant cool of the cabin for the heat of the sun, broiling even at this relatively early hour. The bellhop raised a parasol to offer shade as he guided her inside the building; his colleague busied himself with removing her luggage from the trunk of the limo and wheeling it after them.

She checked in, signing her fake name with a fluent flourish of the pen. The ease befitted something that had become so familiar to her over the years that she sometimes stumbled when signing her real name. The bellhop showed her to the elevator, pressed the button for the fourth floor and made pleasant small talk as they ascended. The floor onto which she emerged was cool and dark, the clamour of the city replaced by the quiet hush of a water feature that had been installed in the elevator lobby. The man opened the door to her suite, wheeled her suitcase inside and delivered a perfunctory explanation of the features of the connecting lounge, bedroom and bathroom. Beatrix thanked him, tipped him with a five thousand-Bolivar note, and waited until the door had closed behind him before taking off her sweaty clothes and stepping into the shower to sluice away the grime of her journey.

She wrapped herself in a towel and unpacked her case. Ops had provided her with it, together with the outfits that Rebecca Smith would wear for her time in the city and those for the trip to the Isla de Margarita that would not happen. Luggage could be opened and checked; the things that were packed inside needed to match her story. She chose a pair of loose-fitting slacks, an airy white blouse, a wide-brimmed sun hat and a pair of Ray-Bans and checked her appearance in the mirror. She looked just as she wanted to look: a businesswoman with pockets deep enough to afford a stylish wardrobe.

She ran her fingers around the inside of the case. There was a tiny incision in the lining, no more than half a centimetre across and almost impossible to see unless you were specifically looking for it. She took a pair of tweezers from her make-up bag and, working with extravagant care, she slid the tips inside the opening and carefully withdrew the SIM card that had been secreted there. She picked up her phone, removed the case, took out the SIM and replaced it with the one that she had removed from her case. She powered up, waited for a signal, and then sent a simple message to acknowledge that she had arrived in Caracas and was commencing the operation. She switched the SIMs again and replaced the secret one back in its hiding place, closed the case and put it away in the wardrobe.

She put the hat on her head, hooked her glasses to the scoop of her blouse, and left the room.

She had an appointment to keep.

Mr. Smith was waiting for her.

Chapter Five

An intelligence officer could not go to a clandestine meeting without first ensuring that he or she was not being followed. They called it 'dry-cleaning', and it usually involved an innocuous cover activity that included a planned route through areas that made it especially difficult to maintain covert surveillance. Beatrix had been given a route and she followed it to the letter: a taxi to the Centro de Arte Los Galpones, an oasis in the heart of the chaotic city, where she wandered through an art gallery and had an iced tea, all the while checking for any signs that she might be followed; and then a second taxi to the Teleférico, the famous cable car system that offered breathtaking views of the capital. Beatrix bought a roundtrip ticket and boarded a car with half a dozen other people, all of whom were tourists unless her instincts were very much awry.

The car took them to the top of the Ávila Mountain. The national park separated the sea from the city, and, as Beatrix stepped out, she was able to breathe the fresh air and relax in the peacefulness of the natural landscape as a counterpoint to the mad bustle of the city. The top of the mountain included a wide promenade along the ridgeline. Sellers had established food and handicraft kiosks, and there was an official restaurant next to an ice skating rink that was promised to open later in the year. An enormous Venezuelan flag snapped in the breeze over the ruins of the old Humboldt Hotel. Low-flying clouds scudded just above the jagged summit of the mountain, and the breeze lent the area a more pleasant temperature, several degrees cooler than the city below.

Beatrix went into the bar and restaurant.

She recognised the man from the photographs in her file. He was of average height and build, his hair cut neat with a lazy comma that hung down over his temple. Not handsome, but not unattractive, either. He was the sort of man who would be able to melt into a crowd without drawing attention to himself. That was a helpful characteristic in this line of work.

"Hello," she said.

He looked up at her.

"John?"

"Yes," he said. "Rebecca?"

"That's right."

"Can I get you a drink, Rebecca?"

"No," she said. "I'm fine."

The opening exchange was designed to confirm identities. Beatrix was satisfied and sat down.

"You been here long?" she asked him.

He looked down at the empty bottles on the table. "Half an hour," he said. She could smell the alcohol on him and suspected it might have been a little longer than that. He wasn't drunk, but it was evident that he had had enough to drink to smooth the edge off the day a little. That was unprofessional, and she noted it for future reference.

"Were you followed?" she asked.

"No," he said. "And you don't need to worry: this isn't my first rodeo."

"No," she said. "I know it isn't."

First impressions—particularly the bottles of beer on the table—were not good. Beatrix knew that Control would ask her for her thoughts on a potential recruit and, at least right now, she didn't anticipate being able to recommend him.

"What's next?" he asked her.

"Have you memorised your legend?"

He nodded. "My name is John Smith," he said. "My wife and I are the principals of Boutique Getaways. We're here to meet with hoteliers on the Isla de Margarita. We are looking for destinations that we can add to our brochure. I've been in Costa Rica and Ecuador, and we scheduled to meet here. Legitimate meetings with hotels on the island were established six weeks ago. I'm quite looking forward to that."

"They won't be going ahead," Beatrix said. "Our son's boarding school will contact us in three days' time. Jasper is going to contract glandular fever and we're going to have to cancel our vacation and return home."

"Jasper?" Milton said. "Jesus, who came up with that?"

Beatrix fixed him with a steely eye; perhaps he was more drunk than she had initially believed. "This isn't a joke," she said. "Have you done anything like this before?"

"Not quite like this," he admitted. "I'm a soldier, not a spy."

That was true; there was a world of difference between what they both did. "Do you know why you were selected for this?"

"I can think of two reasons. Because I've worked down here before."

"That's right," she said. "And the second?"

"My father."

James Milton had enjoyed a successful career in the petrochemical industry, and his success had meant that his family had been forced to endure a peripatetic existence until his retirement. Milton's SIS file recorded stays in Saudi Arabia, Egypt, Dubai and Oman. He had been to Venezuela, too. His history meant that he was conversant in key languages and credible when he spoke about the country.

"Yes," she said. "And there's a third reason, too. Because your commanding officer speaks very highly of you. This is an important assignment. It's also an opportunity for you. If you do a good job, there could be openings for you. The agency that I work for is always looking for operators we can trust."

Milton smiled. "I'm quite happy doing what I'm doing," he said. "Like I said, I'm a soldier, not a spy. This suits me. You'll get one hundred per cent commitment from me, but I can't imagine I'd be interested in a change of career. No offence meant."

His eyes were a crisp, alpine blue, and Beatrix felt uneasy as she looked into them. They were unsettling.

"None taken," she said, quite sure now that she would remove him from Control's list as soon as she returned to London.

"What's next?"

"We're staying at the Cayena. Room 403. Go and check in. I'll meet you there. We'll debrief properly tonight."

Chapter Six

Beatrix spent the rest of the afternoon acclimatising herself to the city. She liked to get a feel for the rhythms and routines of a place, so she wandered the streets like a tourist and soaked everything up. She visited the Jardín de las Piedras Marinas Soñadoras and enjoyed the peace and quiet away from the bustle of the city; she took in the Museo de Bellas Artes, using the quiet galleries to confirm once again that she was not being followed; and she finished her afternoon at El Museo de los Niños, a series of galleries that were designed for children. She wandered the rooms, looking at the exhibits of toys and the interactive displays that delighted the children that were engaging with them, parents and teachers watching behind them as they played. She caught herself daydreaming, the conversation with Wells and then Lucas's consoling words returning to her, and she forced herself to move on.

As the afternoon drew to a close, she stopped to eat an *arepa*—corn flour bread that was served with beef—and then took a taxi back to the hotel.

Milton was waiting for her. He had set himself up on the sofa.

She went into the bathroom and changed out of her hot clothes, choosing a T-shirt and a pair of shorts to replace them. Milton was standing at the minibar when she returned to the main room.

"Want a beer?"

"No, thanks," she said, shooting him a disapproving look as he popped the top off a bottle of Solera, a local brew.

Beatrix sat down. "I need your report," she said. "We need to work out the best way to go about this. What do you know?"

Milton took a slug of the beer and then sat down in the armchair.

"Okay," he said. "So—I've been here three days. The intel was excellent. I found Koralev right away. He comes into the city every morning and has breakfast at Danubio on Mata de Coco. Sunday, yesterday and today, the same time all three days. Eight thirty on the dot. I've been able to follow him afterwards, too. He's not experienced. I'm confident he hasn't made me."

"Confident?"

"I'm sure he hasn't," he said.

"His routine?"

"Breakfast for an hour. Then he goes and buys a newspaper and reads it on the terrace of a coffee shop on Avenida Mohedano. Stays there for an hour, then goes for a walk in the Jardín Hidrofítico. He got into his car and went home after that on Sunday. But yesterday he had a meeting. He went to the observatory in the park and met a man there."

"Any idea who?"

"No. And he struck me as much more careful than Koralev. He was very itchy—he kept his eyes open all the way through the meeting, checking around him. I decided to follow him rather than Koralev when they were finished, but he shook me off quickly. Standard counter-surveillance tactics—it was just me on his tail. No way I could stay on him."

"Pictures?"

"Like I said—not my first rodeo," Milton said.

He reached into his pocket and took out a pack of photographs. He handed them to Beatrix. She looked through the pictures and saw a series that had been taken with the Planetario Humboldt as the backdrop. A man whom Beatrix recognised as Igor Koralev was talking to another younger man. This second man was unshaven and wearing thick black-framed glasses and a cap that Beatrix immediately suspected was part of a disguise. The cap bore a logo on the front that Beatrix vaguely remembered: curved prongs that joined at the top to form the outline of the letter A.

"How long did they talk for?"

"Thirty minutes," Milton said. "I couldn't get close enough to get an idea what they were talking about. It looked intense."

She put the photographs down. "The file says he lives out of town?"

"He does. There's a small village thirty minutes south of Caracas. Cortada de Maturín. You go through it until you get to a private track. It goes up into the hills. You wouldn't be able to follow him without being seen. I was going to hike up there—we could still do that if you wanted to. I staked it out for three hours last night after he went back and then I picked him up as he left this morning. One other car came out last night. It was driven by an old woman. I followed her back to the village. I'm thinking she might be his housekeeper. Nothing else in, nothing else out. It's a good place to hide out."

"Any sign of other meetings?"

Milton shook his head.

"What about protection?"

"No," Milton said, shaking his head. "I don't think he has any. I looked, but I couldn't see anyone."

"He's out here on his own? Just wandering around?"

"As far as I could tell," Milton said.

Beatrix frowned.

"I know what the intel said," Milton said. "But I would have spotted it."

That was entirely consistent with what the briefing had suggested. Beatrix didn't like surprises, but, on the other hand, the job of taking him might have become a lot more straightforward.

"What do you want to do?" Milton said.

"We find him tomorrow. Where would be the best place to take him?"

"The road out of Cortada de Maturín. It's very, very quiet. Not much more than a track until it gets to the Autopista, but that's the main route into the city. It's busy as soon as you hit it."

"We'll pick him up outside the village, then. We'll need a vehicle."

"I've already got one," he said. "I picked one up in town yesterday."

"And weapons?"

"That's sorted, too. I visited the cache yesterday."

Beatrix remembered the file. A Group Fifteen quartermaster had established a small arms cache in a lock-up garage on the west of the city.

"What do you have?"

"Pistols," he said. "There's more in the cache if we need it. It's well equipped. SMGs, grenades, tons of ammo. I didn't think we'd need to go big."

"No," she agreed. "We do it quiet. You have a pistol for me?"

"A Glock 26," he said. "That okay?"

"There wasn't anything else?"

"You don't like it?"

"Not a big fan of polymer frames."

"There's plenty of choice. I could go back and—"

"Forget it. It'll do."

"It's in the car."

She nodded. "What's the inside of the cache like?"

"It's a garage. If you're asking because you want to take him there, I'd say it'd be fine for that. You can drive the car inside and close the door. If he's down in the back, no one would see him."

Beatrix nodded her approval. "That's what we'll do, then. We pick him up, take him to the garage, and have a chat with him."

"A chat?"

"Use your imagination, Major. There are some questions I need him to answer. He might not like all of them."

"I'm sure you can be very persuasive," Milton said.

Beatrix ignored that. "Then we take him to the

coast and get him out of the country."

"And then?"

"And then you go home, with my gratitude and the pride that you can take from a job well done."

Milton stood. He reached down for the beer and took a long draught of it. "If it's all right with you, I'm going to go for a run. Clear my head. You want to get dinner afterwards?"

"No," Beatrix said. "We need to be up early." She pointed at the bottle. "So make that the last one. I do not want you nursing a hangover tomorrow morning."

Milton grinned at her. "No, ma'am."

Chapter Seven

Beatrix was awake with the dawn. She showered and dressed in a pair of dark jeans and a black T-shirt with sleeves that were cut off just below the shoulders. She chose a pair of boots and a light jacket that would hide a pistol if she carried it in her waistband.

Beatrix had gone to bed at nine. Milton hadn't returned to the room, but he had been there when she had risen for a drink in the early hours. He was asleep on the sofa, lying on his back with the covers pulled back to reveal a tattoo of an angel's wings across his shoulders. She had paused close to him; she thought that she could detect the faint smell of alcohol, and his breath was deep and even, a rattle in his throat that was close to snoring. She couldn't tell if he had been out drinking, but, if she had been asked to guess, she would have said that he had. He made no reference to it when he awoke, and, after a shower, he was fresh and ready to work.

He had hired a Opel Vivaro from an agency in Caracas. It was new, and he still hadn't removed the tag that hung down from the stem of the rear-view mirror. It had a sliding door in the side that offered access to a generous cabin. It was a good choice. They would easily be able to get Koralev inside, assuming that Milton's report about his routine—and particularly the assumption that he didn't have close protection—proved to be accurate.

Beatrix sat in the back as Milton drove them out of the city. It was half past six in the morning and the roads were quiet. Beatrix had the Glock on the seat next to her. She made sure that it was unloaded and then disassembled it so that she could check its workings and ensure that everything was clean.

"How long?" Beatrix said.

"Twenty minutes," he said.

The sun was almost all of the way above the horizon now, and the early warmth promised a hot day. Beatrix put the weapon back together again and then tested the trigger. The Glock needed a long trigger pull, with a heavier weight to trigger a round than she preferred. Her favoured weapons employed crisp and clean triggers, and the Glock did not offer that. It wasn't ideal, but that would only become a factor if they needed to fire and, from what Milton had suggested, that shouldn't be necessary.

She pushed the magazine into the grip, racked the slide to load a live round into the chamber and holstered the weapon. She leaned back in the seat and waited.

#

They drove through Cortada de Maturín. It was a sleepy village with a collection of buildings gathered on either side of the road. Milton drove on to the private track that he had mentioned, paused there for Beatrix to assess it, and then turned around and retraced their route. They stopped again to the south of the hamlet, on the other side of a sharp bend that would give Koralev very little time to react once he realised that the way ahead was blocked.

Beatrix had conducted these types of snatch operations many times during her service with the Group. If done properly, they were simple: taking someone off a city street was as easy as clicking your fingers, and doing it on a road like this—with very little chance of being observed—was easier still. The trick was to be quick and efficient. There was no need to make a show. With most targets, the surprise of an abduction rendered them immobile for the small window of time where there would be something that they could do about it.

There was a farmer's field to the left, and it rose to a ridge that offered a view of the surrounding countryside, including the road out of the village. Milton had climbed the ridge with a pair of binoculars that he had taken from the back of the people carrier. They each had a radio and, just a little after eight, Beatrix heard his voice.

"He's coming. Two minutes."

"Copy that."

She glanced up at the ridge and saw Milton making his way down. He picked his way carefully down the steeper sections and then fell into a quick jog so that he would be at the road in time to make the snatch.

Beatrix moved the big Vivaro out into the centre of the road, blocking the way ahead, and left the engine running. She stepped outside. The Glock was shoved in the waistband of her trousers, hidden beneath the back of her loose jacket. A car came around the bend. It was a sharp turn, and the driver had taken it carefully. He was doing only twenty or thirty miles an hour, and he had ample space to stop safely.

Beatrix looked: the sun was reflecting off the windshield, making it difficult for her to see inside. She waved a hand and put a big smile on her face.

The car slowed to a stop.

Beatrix walked forward and stopped before it. If the driver wanted to talk to her, he would have to get out.

Milton closed in, approaching from the rear.

The driver's door opened and a man stepped out.

She could see him now. It was Igor Koralev.

"*Hola?*" he said. "*Puedo ayudarte?*"

His Spanish was atrocious. Beatrix shrugged that she didn't understand, her hand reaching around to the gun and pulling it just as Milton turned the corner around Koralev's car and grabbed him, his own gun pressed to the side of the old man's head. Milton wrapped his left arm around Koralev's neck and half-pushed, half-dragged him to the Vivaro.

Beatrix ran to Koralev's car and moved it into a space at the side of the road. She returned to the Vivaro and got in, drawing the Glock and training it on Koralev.

"Stay on the floor between the seats," she said. "Don't move. Don't talk. If you do what I tell you to do, you'll be fine."

Milton opened the driver's door, put the people carrier into drive, and released the brake.

They set off.

It had taken less than twenty seconds, and no one had seen a thing.

Chapter Eight

Milton drove them to the arms cache in Casalta. The location was an outdoor facility on the fringes of the city that offered long-term storage. There were small- and medium-sized sheds going all the way to larger garages and, as they rolled in off the road, Beatrix saw to her satisfaction that the place was deserted. Koralev was on the floor of the Vivaro. Beatrix had cuffed his wrists behind his back and hooded him with her jacket. She had the muzzle of the gun against the back of his head to persuade him that it was in his best interests to stay where he was. Milton pulled up next to one of the larger units, went outside and unlocked the door. He rolled it up, the metal slats clacking as they folded away, and then reversed the Opel inside. He killed the engine, pulled down the door and switched on a strip light.

Beatrix got out, leaving Koralev on the floor.

The garage was, effectively, an arms dump. The quartermaster had equipped it well. Racking had been screwed to the walls on both sides, and an array of weapons was laid out there. Beatrix saw long guns and pistols, automatic rifles, shotguns, packages of plastique, grenades, and numerous boxes of ammunition. Group Fifteen had caches like this all around the world. Some were smaller: metal crates that were buried in out-of-the-way locations. Others, like this, were established on an ad hoc basis as the need arose. The equipment had most likely been air-dropped or smuggled onto a secluded beach and then transported here. The quartermaster was available to assist should the need arise, but, in most cases, they maintained a scrupulous cover and did little to jeopardise that.

"Not bad," Beatrix said as Milton joined her.

"How do you want to play this?" he asked quietly.

"We'll double-team him," Beatrix said.

"Good cop, bad cop?"

"Yes."

"Who am I?" Milton asked.

"You frighten him," she said. "And then I'll tell him everything will be okay."

"I can do that," he said, and Beatrix saw those icy blue eyes again and believed that he could.

"We need information on what he's been doing here," she said. "He was tempted to leave the States by an offer from someone—we need to know who that is. We need to know where he's been working, what he's been working on, what he's offered to sell."

"And then?"

"We'll see. It depends what he says. But we're still going to repatriate him. The Navy has a frigate waiting twenty miles off shore. They're going to send a vessel to transfer him. There's a smuggler's beach at Puerto Cumarebo. We'll take him there."

"Fine," Milton said. He turned and looked back to the people carrier. "Shall we get started?"

Chapter Nine

They took Koralev out of the Vivaro and dragged him to an old roller chair that had been left at the side of the space. They dumped him on it, his hands still cuffed behind his back and his head still covered by Beatrix's jacket. Milton removed it. Koralev looked up, blinking a little as his eyes adjusted to the light. He was frightened, as well he ought to be; he looked left and right, shooting furtive glances at his surroundings.

"Hello, Igor," Milton said.

The old man didn't speak.

Milton made a show of taking off his jacket, folding it over his arm and then going back to the Vivaro to leave it on the hood. He undid his shirt cuffs and rolled the sleeves up to his elbows.

"I'm afraid you've put yourself in an awkward situation. I work for the British government. Our friends in the Central Intelligence Agency were very upset that you decided to run out on them. They said you were disloyal. Ungrateful, too—that was another word they used to describe you. They invested a lot of money in you and your work, didn't they? I can see why they might be annoyed when they found out that you were trying to sell it to someone else."

"Who are you?" Koralev said in a voice stretched thin by tension.

"My name's not important. All you need to know is that this operation is unofficial. And that's not good for you. It means I'm not constrained by British law. I have a free hand to do whatever I want when it comes to you. Anything."

"I'm an old man, sir," Koralev said. "You don't need to threaten me. I won't fight."

Milton looked over at Beatrix; perhaps this would be easier than they had anticipated. She took out the small voice recorder that she had in her pocket and pressed record. She put the recorder in her pocket and walked around so that she was in front of Koralev's chair. Milton nodded to the door, indicating that he would go and stand watch. Beatrix nodded back and waited for him to push up the door and duck outside.

She turned to Koralev. "Why don't we have a chat? This doesn't need to be unpleasant."

"I am a scientist," he said. "I'm just a scientist." He jerked his head at their surroundings. "None of this is necessary. Just let me go. I just want to go home."

"We both know that I can't do that. The CIA has invested a lot of money into your work. They want you back again."

Koralev slumped farther down into the chair. He had no fight in him at all. "I knew this would happen," he said. "You will take me back?"

"Yes."

"I knew they would never let me go. I can't run. I'm too tired."

Beatrix felt a flutter of sympathy for him. "Are you thirsty?"

"Yes," he said.

There was a bottle of water in the back of the Vivaro.

She collected it and, after removing the cuffs, gave it to him. He drank heartily.

"Thank you," he said.

"I have some questions for you," she said.

Koralev nodded wearily. "I have nothing to hide. Ask me whatever you want."

"Why did you run?"

"You don't know?"

"No," she said.

"Have you heard of the Soviet Biopreparat program?"

Beatrix had never heard of it. "No," she said.

"It goes back years. All the way back to Stalin. The Red Army was crushed in the First World War; then the Nazis killed millions more in the Second. My father died. My mother could barely find the food to feed me and my sister when we were growing up. Stalin wanted to make sure that the motherland was better prepared should a similar conflict arise in the future. He wanted to develop soldiers with advantages that would make them more efficient than the men they faced."

"What kind of advantages?"

"Metabolic ones. Faster. Stronger. More endurance." He coughed and then blew his nose into a handkerchief he took from his pocket. "He started with an embryologist. His name was Vladimir Ivanosky. He had been experimenting on chimpanzees. It didn't work. Then he started working on monkey sperm, trying to impregnate volunteers. That didn't work, either. But they didn't give up."

Beatrix had no idea where Koralev was going with this. She let him talk.

"Biopreparat is a bioweapons program. Chemical weapons. Diseases. Research into all of it. Vladimir worked there for many years, as did his son and then his grandson. The grandson is Nikita Ivanosky—he is also an embryologist. Nikita started to look at monkey DNA, examining how it could be changed."

"How do you know this?" Beatrix asked.

"I am a scientist, as I have said. My own specialism is molecular biology and biophysics. It was the area that Nikita needed the most help with. He was aware of my work, so he recruited me. I say he 'recruited' me—what I mean to say is that he recommended me, and, the next day, two KGB agents visited my university and told me that I had to go with them. I didn't see my family for six months. Nikita and I started to work together. Our program was installed on an island in the Aral Sea, where bioweapons were tested. It lies between Kazakhstan and Uzbekistan. Do you know the area? Do you know what it's like?"

"No," Beatrix said, although she had been there and she did know.

"It is cold and bleak and barren. The island is called Vozrozhdeniya. They tested anthrax there. They tied horses and donkeys to concrete posts and then released the spores to see what would happen. It was not a pleasant place to work."

He took a moment. Beatrix waited for him to go on.

"I became close to Nikita. I persuaded him that we

should take our research to the Americans. I was greedy—I make no excuses for myself. The chaos caused by the Wall coming down meant Moscow was distracted. It made it easier for us to leave. We contacted the CIA and they took us to America. I expect you know what happened next? They gave us money and facilities and let us carry on with our work."

"This was Daedalus?"

"Yes," Koralev said. "A front for the work we were doing. A distraction." He drank again. "We made significant progress," he said. "We had more money than before. An excellent team to help us. World-class facilities. We were able to develop a somatic treatment that produced permanent genetic changes in the subjects. The difficulty was in keeping the subjects alive. They developed cancer and died. The Americans did not give up. They gave us more and more money. And, eventually, we found our success."

"So why did you leave?"

"It's not money," he said. "I have learned my lesson about greed. I have more than I could ever spend. It is…" He paused. "Nikita and I have developed a philosophical difference of opinion. It's fundamental—it means that we can no longer work together. We have been successful beyond our wildest dreams. The work that Daedalus has done will change the way we think about genetics forever. But as we became more successful, it became more obvious to me what our work would mean. I was naïve. I ignored the money they poured into the company. Millions and millions of dollars. I persuaded myself that it was for the good of science, that we would have an influence on how the research was put to use. But…" He paused again and cleared his throat. "But they wanted a return on their investment. They would not listen to me. As soon as we had viable test subjects, the company was pushed in a different direction. The Department of Defense became heavily involved. You have heard of DARPA? The Defense Advanced Research Projects Agency."

"Yes," Beatrix said.

"And Manage Risk? Do you know them?"

"The private military contractors?"

He nodded. "Daedalus was hidden within it. DARPA increased the funding, but the work was buried. They took sixty years of research and they weaponised it. They sent our children into the world to work for them and I decided that I had had enough."

"Your children?"

"The viable test subjects—that is what they call them."

"What does that mean? Testing for what?"

"I told you," he said, as if explaining himself to a small child, "they are seeking metabolic dominance."

Beatrix looked at him. It was difficult not to think that his story was ridiculous. She would have been unable to credit any of it save that, whatever else he said, Koralev's work and his sudden abandonment of it had attracted the attention of the CIA and, in turn, Group Fifteen. Whatever it was that he had done, it had led him to this meeting with her. There was something there, no matter how outlandish his claims. They wouldn't have been involved otherwise. And her assessment of his story was an irrelevance, anyway. She had orders to follow. That was all that mattered.

"So you just left?" she said.

"Yes," he said.

"And no one is paying you to be here?"

"Have I been bought?" he asked. She nodded, and he shook his head. "No. I have been bought before. I want the opposite now. Freedom from that, from having my name associated with all of it. I wanted to leave while I still could. I chose here because they will not send me back. No extradition. And the CIA has no reach here."

Beatrix almost corrected him in that, but checked herself.

The door rolled up. Milton was crouched down outside. "Beatrix," he called out.

She walked across the room toward him. His body was cast in silhouette by the blazing sun. "What is it?"

"We've got trouble."

#

Beatrix joined him at the door.

"Over there," he said. "You see that building. Right-hand side."

She squinted into the brightness. Milton indicated a building on the other side of the yard, near the entrance.

"You see?" Milton asked.

"No."

"There's a man behind the building. I just saw him."

"A customer?"

Milton raised his hand with his finger pointing up and circled it. "He signalled a rally point," he said. "There's more than one of him. And he had a weapon."

She gritted her teeth. "They must have followed us."

"Impossible," he said. "We were thorough."

Beatrix allowed herself a very brief moment to lay out the alternatives. Might Milton have been involved? He was right: they *had* been thorough. But could he have taken this moment of privacy to signal their location? He had been out of her sight for fifteen minutes. It would have been a simple enough thing to power up a tracker, to make a quick call or send a text. She dismissed the thought. They were several miles from the centre of Caracas. It would have taken longer than that to scramble assets to their location. But the thought persisted. Might he have signalled earlier? He had hired the Vivaro. It would have been easy enough to slap a tracker somewhere where she wouldn't see it. She certainly hadn't checked.

She couldn't disregard it, but her gut told her that he was on the level.

"Who do you think it is?" he asked her.

"The Americans?"

"I thought this was a joint op? Why would they come without telling us?"

"Maybe he's too important for them to trust us to deliver him."

"Could be the people he's been working for," he suggested.

"He says he's not working for anyone," she said. "It doesn't matter. I'm not waiting to find out."

"What is it?" Koralev called from inside.

Beatrix and Milton slipped inside the garage again.

"We're leaving," Beatrix said to Koralev.

"Why?"

She went over to him and helped him up from the chair. His age made his bones stiff. He clutched her arm for support.

"Load up," she called over to Milton. "Firearms, grenades, ammunition, anything else that you can quickly get into the back."

She opened the door of the Vivaro and helped Koralev climb inside.

"Who is it?" the old man said.

"I'm not sure," Beatrix said. "But we're not going to wait to find out."

He didn't complain. He sat quietly in the minivan, rubbing his wrists where they had been chafed by the cuffs. Beatrix looked at him and wished that they had a little more time.

"Fasten your seat belt," she told him."

Milton started to toss equipment from the racks inside: a big rifle, an MP5 SMG, a carrying case for a pistol, a bandolier of grenades, night-vision goggles, ammunition. Satisfied, he yanked the door shut. "Here," he said, tossing the MP5 over to her.

"Thanks," she said. "I'll drive. You ride shotgun. Open the door."

Milton jogged around and rolled the door all the way up to the top. Sunlight streamed inside the garage;

Beatrix squinted out into it, still unable to see any sign of the men Milton believed were outside. He joined her in the people carrier. Beatrix put her hand on the ignition.

"You ready?"

Milton had chosen an AR-10. It was a big machine gun that fired a 7.62mm cartridge; a nice, heavy bullet. He flicked the selector to full auto.

"Ready," he said.

She turned the key.

Chapter Ten

Beatrix floored the gas. The tyres bit on the concrete floor and she had to wrestle the wheel straight as the Vivaro lurched from side to side.

The lookout that Milton had noticed saw them first. Beatrix saw him running as they came out of the door. He was wearing black from head to foot, with a balaclava on his head and black gloves. He held a short submachine gun.

The only way out of the yard was to pass directly by the building that the lookout had used for shelter. There was just enough space to fit the people carrier between the building and an old railway carriage that had been dumped there. It would have been an excellent choke point, but Beatrix and Milton had reacted before the blockade had been arranged. They raced through the gap, jolting and juddering across the uneven ground and passing the running man at forty.

They came out from between the buildings and onto the open space that led to the road. She saw them all now. An assault team was mustering, disembarking from two vans and two SUVs, all four vehicles equipped with tinted windows. They must have heard the sound of the approaching vehicle since Beatrix was driving it at high revs; indeed, they had evidently been warned by the lookout that Milton had spotted.

The parked vehicles blocked the direct route out of the yard and onto the road. Beatrix slammed on the brakes and spun the wheel hard to the left, sliding the unwieldy minivan around so that Milton's window faced the collection of men and vehicles. She stomped on the gas, the wheels biting in the grit and dirt and sending a spray up behind them.

Milton pressed the AR-10's stock into his shoulder, aimed out of the window and fired. The gun roared and a dozen big 7.62mm rounds streamed out. The muzzle brake reduced the kick and made it possible to handle, even in a vehicle that was moving at speed. Milton aimed at the vehicles, peppering them with bullets. Tyres exploded, gouts of steam jetted from pierced radiators and glass flew out of windows. The men dived for cover as Beatrix yanked the wheel in the opposite direction, the tyres carving lazy curves in the grit as she swung the rear end around and pointed at the suddenly accessible path to the exit.

"Covering fire!" she yelled, but Milton had already replaced the magazine and was out of the window again, this time pointing behind them.

The AR-10 roared as Milton emptied the second magazine, a third in his lap ready to be slapped in when the second ran dry. Beatrix looked into the rear-view mirror as one of the SUVs exploded, its fuel tank ignited by one of his rounds.

They raced out of the exit. Beatrix flicked her eyes back to the road ahead just as another blacked-out SUV raced right at them. There was no time to avoid it. The vehicle clipped them on the front right wing, swinging them around to the left, turning through one hundred and eighty degrees so that the nose of their vehicle was pointing back into the yard. Milton was slammed against the door by the impact, his grip on the rifle lost as he fumbled it into his lap. Beatrix jackknifed forward, her forehead bouncing against the dashboard. She fought a moment of dizziness and tasted her own blood in her mouth.

She grabbed the MP5 and aimed through the windshield at the vehicle that had struck them. The SUV had been turned onto its right-hand side by the impact and had skidded for another twenty feet along the road. It ground to a halt, a torn-off wing and a scattering of broken glass discarded in its wake. It had swung around a few degrees and Beatrix could see its underside, the suspension and covers. The two wheels that were off the ground were still spinning.

She heard a loud thud and then another.

She watched as the nearside door of the SUV, buckled by the impact, was forced open.

She saw a hand grasping the sill and then a head and shoulders emerge.

"Get down!"

She turned back to look out of the windshield and saw the two men as Milton yelled his warning. They emerged from behind the burning SUV in the yard with their rifles raised. The windshield exploded over them both as a hail of gunfire converged on them, taking out the glass and exiting through the rear window and holes that were punched in the roof. Milton and Beatrix were down below the line of the windshield, with partial protection from the engine block ahead of them. She threw the Vivaro into reverse, stomped on the gas and yanked the wheel, operating blind and entirely on instinct. She realigned the people carrier, skidding back through ninety degrees so that she was pointing down the road.

"*Hit it!*"

She jammed it into first, hit the gas again, and risked a glance back into the yard as they jerked away.

She checked the wing mirror, expecting to see the two men chasing after them from the yard, but her attention was taken by a figure atop the overturned SUV. It was a man and he, too, was dressed all in black.

The man jumped down from the wreck, landing lightly on the balls of his feet, and then he started to run.

Beatrix changed up into second. They reached the pocked asphalt, the tyres gripped, and they started to pull away.

She checked the mirror.

The man was still running.

He reached to a holster that crisscrossed his chest and pulled out a handgun.

"*Milton!*" Beatrix yelled.

Beatrix looked back to the road ahead as a large flatbed truck rumbled out of another exit to the yard. It was slowly turning away from them, the tractor angled sharply as the trailer followed suit. It blocked the road. Beatrix hammered on the brake and swung the wheel to the left, bleeding away enough speed so that she was able to swerve around the obstruction. The Vivaro left the road, bouncing over a raised lip of sun-hardened dirt and crashing down onto a flat expanse of loose gravel and scree.

Beatrix swung the wheel to the right and changed down into first. She looked into the mirror.

They had lost speed and the man had gained on them.

"Take him out!"

Milton swung around, aimed the rifle between the front seats and out of the back of the cabin. Koralev pressed himself against the door and covered his head with both arms as Milton opened fire. The rifle chugged through the third magazine, the rounds chewing up chunks of road as the rounds sought Milton's target. The man danced to his left and right, zigzagging. None of Milton's rounds found their mark, and the man kept coming.

"I'm dry," Milton yelled.

Beatrix reached for the MP5 in her lap and held it up.

Milton took it.

The man behind them was ten feet away now. He had been sprinting flat out for over three hundred metres and was still maintaining the same speed. Beatrix had never seen anything like it. His endurance was remarkable.

The man raised his own sidearm and started to fire.

The rear side window blew into the cabin. Beatrix felt the hot rush of a round as it passed close by her head, slicing through the already perforated roof. Two more chinged against the bodywork. A rear airbag detonated, the air exploding out of it almost as soon as it had inflated as a second round punctured it. Blue talc from the deployment mechanism sifted into the interior. The people carrier slewed to the side, Beatrix fighting hard to keep it pointing ahead.

The man had caught them up. He was alongside now.

Milton aimed the MP5 at her.

"Down!"

Beatrix did as he asked, lowering her head between her arms and driving blind. The muzzle of the submachine gun was close to her ear and its roar was deafening as Milton loosed an automatic volley. When Beatrix raised her head and glanced into the mirror, she saw their pursuer lying flat on his back, his arms splayed out wide, a crucifix facing up into the sky.

"Go, go, go," Milton urged.

Beatrix yanked the wheel around again, bounced over the raised lip of hardened dirt and bounced onto the road once more. She changed up to second and then to third and, still accelerating, she drove them away from the yard.

Chapter Eleven

Beatrix raced ahead, aiming to the west and the start of the run to the exfiltration point on the coast. The wind rushed in through the open space where the windshield had been. She caught a glimpse of her lap: she was covered in glass, large jagged jigsaw pieces and tiny fragments that glittered like diamonds on a velvet cushion.

She glanced across at Milton. "You okay?"

"Yes," he said.

Beatrix glanced into the rear-view.

"Koralev?"

The old man was leaning at an angle, held up by his seat belt.

"Koralev?" she repeated. "Check him."

Milton swung around in his seat. "Shit."

"What is it?"

"He's been hit. Just below his shoulder."

Beatrix cursed, slapping both hands against the wheel.

"It's bad," Milton added.

She looked ahead. They were approaching Hoyo de la Puerta. There was a slip road that exited Route 1 and she took it, turning on to the much quieter El Café Road. There was a hotel with a large parking lot. Beatrix turned into it and parked the Vivaro between two larger vehicles. They would have had to stop, anyway. The vehicle had no windshield, and the wing and hood had been perforated so many times that they looked like Swiss cheese. It was hardly inconspicuous.

She switched off the engine, opened the door and went around so that she could slide in next to the old man. Milton was right: a round had struck him halfway between his pectoral muscle and clavicle. His shirt was already sodden with warm blood and his breathing hissed in and out in frequent, hungry gulps.

Beatrix made an immediate diagnosis: his lung had been punctured and was in danger of collapsing.

She told Milton to get her the duct tape that she had seen in the back of the people carrier and ripped open the old man's shirt. She would try to delay the process by creating a one-way valve. She needed to stop air from getting sucked into Koralev's chest through the wound as he breathed in, yet still allow excess air to escape through the bullet hole. She tore off two pieces of tape and stuck them together so that there was no sticky side and then placed it over the entry wound. She taped down three sides, doing so loosely so that there was a little slack. She left one side open and then checked. Whenever Koralev inhaled, the valve lid was sucked down to seal the wound so that air could not get in. When he exhaled, excess air from the chest pushed up the lid so that it could escape through the edge that was not taped down. It was makeshift, and far from perfect, but it might buy him a few extra minutes.

Koralev reached for her, his hand falling limply on her elbow. His mouth opened and closed and she realised that he was trying to speak.

"Phoenix," he said.

"Hold on," Beatrix said. "We're going to get you a doctor."

Milton opened the passenger door and went around to retrieve the gear.

Koralev shook his head. "No. No doctor. Not that."

He coughed.

She leaned closer. "What then?"

He grunted with pain, taking a long breath until he had mastered it. "There is a house. Cortada de Maturín. There is a track on the road to the north of the town."

"Is that your house?" she asked. "We've seen the track."

He nodded. "Take it. It goes into the mountains. The house… the house is a mile later."

"You want me to go there?"

He nodded again.

"Why?"

"My work. Everything is there."

"Okay," she said. "I'll get it. What is it? A computer?"

He didn't answer. "There is a person on the Internet. He believes… freedom of information. He will publish it. If we spread it wide"—he coughed violently—"if everyone sees it, they will understand what we have done. The monsters we have created. People will understand what Daedalus is trying to do. And then, perhaps, they will be forced to stop."

His skin, already pale, was becoming tinged with blue. He wasn't getting enough oxygen.

"Stay with me," Beatrix urged.

"Phoenix," Koralev said weakly.

"What?"

"Phoenix is there."

"What is Phoenix?"

"You must... must..."

The words sighed away into nothing.

"Igor," she said, shaking him gently.

There was no answer.

The scientist's eyes were closed.

"Shit."

"Is he dead?" Milton asked.

"No. Still breathing. But he can't have long."

"What do we do?"

"We can't exfiltrate him like this—he won't make it to the pickup. He needs a doctor."

Milton shook his head. "We can't take him to a hospital—"

"I know we can't," Beatrix snapped, cutting him off. "Call the quartermaster. He'll have a re-tread you can take him to."

She had decided at the weapons cache that it was already past time for them to go their separate ways. The information that Koralev had just provided was another reason why that was necessary: they had no choice now but to split up.

"And then?" Milton asked.

"If he makes it, get him out of the country, as per the plan. If he doesn't make it, get yourself out. Call London. Keep them in the picture."

"What about you?"

"I have two sets of orders. Get Igor. Done that."

"And then?"

"Find answers." She looked up into the bright morning sky. "That's what I'm going to do."

Chapter Twelve

They left the Vivaro in the car park and stole two replacements. Milton took a Ford Explorer and Beatrix a Jeep Grand Cherokee. Koralev was still alive when they carefully loaded him into the back of the Ford, but Beatrix did not expect him to make it. He was losing blood, his breathing shallow and pitiful. But she decided that they would try to save him, however futile the attempt.

Beatrix transferred the equipment from the Vivaro to the Jeep and then watched as Milton pulled out of the lot. She followed behind. Milton raised his hand as he turned to the north. Beatrix returned the gesture, doubting that she would see him again. She turned in the other direction, to the south.

#

Cortada de Maturín was thirty minutes south of Caracas and just twenty minutes from the parking lot of the hotel. Beatrix was careful to stay at the speed limit. She had the MP5 on the seat next to her and she had no intention of being stopped by the police for driving too fast.

She exited the Autopista and followed a narrow road that ascended into hilly terrain. Cortada was a small hamlet, not even big enough to be described as a village, and she passed through it until she was on the northern boundary. She continued for another minute until she saw a turning to her right. It was little more than a dirt track through the trees. She slowed down and turned onto the track, grateful for the rugged vehicle as she bounced and jumped across the uneven surface. She followed the road for a mile, just as Koralev had instructed.

She slowed to a stop. The track ascended higher into the hills, bending around a lazy curve as it climbed. There was a switchback above her, and, nestled within the serpentine left-hand swing of the track, she saw a house.

#

Beatrix parked the car within the shelter afforded by a cleft in the track and, following the treeline, moved to within fifty metres of the property. She scouted ahead with the binoculars from the cache. The house was compact, with the windows on the first floor suggesting two or three bedrooms. There was a garden with a raised vegetable patch. A child's colourful paddling pool. The property stood in a position that afforded it a panoramic view into the valley through which Beatrix had approached. It looked small and pleasant.

There were two cars parked next to the house. Beatrix focused on them: one was an old Peugeot; the other was a Cadillac Escalade with blackout windows.

Beatrix waited, surveilling the cars with the binoculars. The Peugeot was empty, but the door of the Escalade opened and a woman stepped outside. Beatrix was too far away to make out fine details, even with the binoculars, save that the woman was wearing a skirt and jacket. She crossed the space between the Cadillac and the house and knocked on the door.

Beatrix pressed the glasses to her eyes and held her breath.

The door opened. Another woman stood inside the threshold; again, detail was hard to make out, but Beatrix could see that she was older and wearing an apron.

A conversation took place. Beatrix watched for a moment: the woman in the doorway shook her head, raising her hands in front of her as if to deflect whatever it was that the younger woman was saying.

Beatrix thought that she saw something from the Escalade. She quickly turned the binoculars back to the vehicle as a door on the opposite side of the vehicle opened and a man stepped out.

She looked back to the conversation at the front door just as the younger woman reached a hand into her jacket and then extended her arm straight out in front of her. Beatrix saw the flash of a gunshot and then heard the muffled report from a suppressed pistol. The older woman fell back into the house, just her legs visible as they poked out of the door.

Two more men emerged from the Escalade.

That made four enemies: the woman and three male associates.

The woman went inside, followed by the three men.

Beatrix waited a moment to compose herself. She adjusted the MP5 on its strap for better accessibility and then started toward the house.

Chapter Thirteen

Beatrix stayed in the cover of the treeline until she was adjacent to the house and then paused again to take stock. One of the windows on the ground floor of the house faced her, and she was able to look inside with the binoculars. She saw a flash of movement as a figure wearing black moved around inside.

She reached down for the MP5's pistol grip and scurried across the track until she was able to press herself against the side of the Escalade. She paused in its shelter, hidden from the house, and listened hard. Nothing, just the singing of the birds. She peered around the open door of the Cadillac so that she could see inside the cabin.

The vehicle was empty.

She edged along the body of the SUV until she was at a vantage point that allowed her to look around the rear to the open door of the house. The body of the older woman had been moved farther inside. A man in black clothes moved across the open doorway; he had a weapon in his hand.

Beatrix waited until he was out of sight and then crossed the space between the vehicle and the house. She pressed her back against the stone wall next to the door and listened. Cradling the MP5 in both hands, she took a deep breath and then put her head around the edge of the door so that she could look inside.

It was a kitchen: there was a table, an American-style refrigerator, and an old washing machine that had seen better days. The old woman's body had been dumped next to a kitchen table, her legs splayed, her arms limp at her side, blood running from the fresh wound in the centre of her forehead.

Beatrix crouched low and slipped inside. She could hear people upstairs: the sound of feet on creaking floorboards and low voices. She crossed the kitchen to a door that opened onto a hallway but, before she was halfway there, she heard feet descending a flight of stairs. She diverted, sliding behind the open door. The kitchen counter was to her left and there was a knife block within reach. She left the machine pistol to hang on its strap, took a large chef's knife and held it in her right fist.

The footsteps reached the bottom of the stairs and came toward the kitchen.

Beatrix gripped the knife tight and raised it to head height.

One of the three men came through the door and into the kitchen. He was wearing a shoulder rig, the leather straps crossing over his back with the holster and a magazine pouch beneath his armpits.

He didn't see Beatrix. She ghosted out of her hiding place, reached up to snag his hair with her left fist, yanked back on his head to expose his throat and then, before he even had time to draw the breath for a warning shout, she brought her right hand up and sliced through his throat with the blade. His body went limp; Beatrix dropped her left arm so that she could loop it beneath his left shoulder and clasped him around the chest. She dragged him to the side so that he wouldn't be visible from the open doorway through which he had just emerged.

One down.

Three left.

Beatrix left the bloodied knife on the counter and crept back to the doorway. There was a hallway, with two doors to the side and a flight of stairs that ascended to the first floor. She quickly cleared the ground floor rooms: there was a small sitting room and a bathroom, both empty. She came back into the hall and started up the stairs.

And then she stopped.

A noise.

Distinctive and unmistakeable.

The sound of a baby's crying.

She paused, trying to place it. The noise was muffled, as if passing through a closed door.

Beatrix held her breath.

The baby cried out again.

Upstairs.

She started to climb the stairs again, pausing just before she reached the top.

The stairs opened onto a landing. There was a door to the right and two to the left.

She risked a glance around the corner. The door to the right was open, and the room beyond was empty. It had bare floorboards and there were empty cardboard boxes stacked up against the wall.

She swung back behind the wall, took a breath, and readied herself.

She switched the machine pistol to three-shot burst mode and gripped it hard, almost as if she was twisting both hands to keep her elbows tight into her torso. She stepped out of the stairwell, turning to the left and holding herself in a line-backer stance, one foot slightly ahead of the other, and squared up to the two open doors.

Two bedrooms.

One of the men was in the bedroom to her right and the other was in the room to her left. The one on the left was facing away, and so she took aim first at his colleague. She held herself in a strong stance, her right foot slightly behind her left for the additional support that she needed when firing. Beatrix pulled the trigger. She had the luxury of an aimed burst, and all three rounds found their target. The man went down.

Beatrix swivelled and took aim at the second man. The rattle of the MP5 had startled him into turning, and he was halfway around as Beatrix fired again. Her stance was solid enough that she was able to hold the machine pistol with no muzzle rise, and that ensured that her accuracy was good. She fired a second three-round burst: he was side-on, showing a narrow profile, and two of the shots found their mark. The third missed, blasting through a window, the glass falling down into the yard below.

Beatrix heard the baby's cry again and advanced toward it, moving carefully into the room where she had just shot the second man. It wasn't a bedroom, she realized: it was a nursery. A crib sat beneath a mobile of fluffy miniature animals that turned in the breeze that was blowing in from the shattered window.

The woman was there, in the corner. She had a baby in her arms. Her pistol was in a shoulder holster and her grasp of the baby to her chest meant that she was unable to reach for it.

"Don't move," Beatrix said.

The woman stepped back until she was against the wall, with nowhere else to go.

"Who are you?" Beatrix asked.

The woman didn't answer.

Beatrix glanced at the man on the floor. One of the two bullets that had struck him had caught him in the side of the head; he would have been dead before he hit the floor. Beatrix couldn't hear anything from the second bedroom. That man, too, could be safely assumed to be incapacitated.

Three down.

One left.

It was just her and this woman now.

"Put the baby down."

"You don't know what you're doing," the woman said. She spoke in a clear, uninflected voice. No accent that Beatrix could place.

Beatrix's mouth was dry and she felt a moment of weakness that was unfamiliar to her. She swallowed, trying to get moisture into her mouth, but it was no good. The baby gazed at her.

"Put the baby down."

The woman stared at her. "You're making a mistake."

"Last chance. Three."

"Who sent you?" the woman asked.

Beatrix ignored the question. "Two."

"Speak to them," the woman urged.

"One—"

"Okay, okay," the woman said

She started to lower the baby to the crib, but, before she reached it, she dropped the infant the rest of the way and reached for her pistol.

Beatrix pulled the trigger for a third time. The room was small, and Beatrix was too close to miss. All three bullets peppered the woman in a diagonal from the right shoulder down to the left hip. The impacts staggered her. She fell against the wall and then slumped down to a sitting position.

Beatrix approached, the muzzle of the machine pistol aimed at her head.

The woman looked up her, coughed up a mouthful of crimson blood, sighed once, and then was still. Beatrix closed the distance until she was close enough to remove the pistol from the holster. She put it aside and frisked the woman. There was nothing: no phone, no form of identification, nothing that might leave any clue as to who she was.

The baby cried out again. Beatrix stood and looked down into the crib. The child was tiny. Beatrix was no judge, but she would have guessed that it was seven or eight months old, surely no older than that. A girl? She thought so. She had been lucky, landing on the blankets and, beneath them, a thin mattress.

She reached her hands beneath the baby's body, so small and fragile that her fingertips touched behind its back. She lifted it out of the bed; the blanket snagged and came away from the crib, too. The baby was warm and, as she dipped her face closer, she could smell it. There was no reason for it, but she was put in mind of warm biscuits and milk.

Beatrix was buffeted by a dizzying sensation that took her completely by surprise.

The child gazed up at her. She cradled it, holding out a finger. The baby reached for it, one tiny hand fixing around it. Beatrix looked down. It was definitely a girl. She was wearing a pink suit that left her arms and legs bare. She had a head of fine blond hair, round cheeks, and arms and legs that looked like fattened sausages.

"What's your name?"

The baby kept looking at her. She didn't smile, but they maintained eye contact for a long moment. Beatrix felt naked, as if the little girl were able to penetrate her deceptions, mistruths and diversions to divine her true thoughts. Beatrix found it unsettling, and for that moment, she was lost. Then, out of the corner of her eye, she saw movement. She looked through the window, down to the base of the valley. Shifting the child to the crook of her left arm, she raised the binoculars with her right hand and saw a black SUV that twisted and turned as it negotiated the bends that presaged the climb up to the house.

Reinforcements.

Beatrix reached for the MP5. Clutching the baby close, and with the submachine gun suspended by its strap, she turned for the door.

Part Two

Chapter Fourteen

Beatrix Rose found herself kept waiting in the room outside Control's office for the second time in a week. She had been asked to meet him for the usual debrief at three, and it was a quarter to four the last time she had checked her watch. Captain Tanner was his usual apologetic self, mouthing that he was sorry as he closed the door to the office behind him and retook his seat.

For once, Beatrix didn't mind. She had a lot to occupy her thoughts.

The light above the door changed from red to green.

"You can go through now, Number One," said Tanner.

Beatrix stood, straightened her jacket, and went to the door.

#

Beatrix went inside and closed the door behind her. Control was at his desk. There was another man in the room, too. He was sitting in one of the generous club chairs by the fireplace. He was in his sixties, with leathery skin and rheumy eyes that bulged behind thick-rimmed spectacles. He dressed badly, like a rural vicar: a tweed jacket and brown cord trousers that were frayed at the cuffs. He had a bound file in his lap. Beatrix recognised a copy of her report.

"Ah," said Control. "Good afternoon, Number One."

"Sir."

Control gestured to the second man. "This is Vivian Bloom," he said. "Works for SIS. He was involved with planning the operation."

"Indeed," Bloom said. "I wanted to hear your report myself. And to thank you for a job well done."

Beatrix regarded him more closely. His tie was stained and the collar of his shirt curled up at the edges. She had never seen anyone who worked for SIS who looked anything like him. "Thank you, sir."

Control tapped his finger on the bound document on his desk. "I've read your report, Beatrix. Very thorough, as usual."

"Thank you, sir. Can I ask about the attack at the arms cache? Do we know who that was?"

"We don't," Bloom said. "We're still looking into it. I know Koralev told you he wasn't working for anyone, but, frankly, I don't buy that. Doesn't make sense. Our working hypothesis is that it was an attempt to get him back."

"So why wasn't he protected? We were able to take him off the street with no opposition."

"I can't answer that, Miss Rose," Bloom said.

"Seems odd that they would leave him unprotected and then go to such lengths to get him back."

"It does, I agree. As yet, we're no closer to why that might be. We're investigating."

"What about Koralev and Major Milton?" Beatrix said.

"You don't know?"

"No," she said.

"Koralev died in the car before Milton could get him to a doctor."

"He was in bad shape," she said.

"Quite. A shame we couldn't get him out."

Was that a slight? She ignored it. "What about Major Milton?"

"Picture-perfect extraction," Control said. "He made his way to Puerto Cumarebo and the Navy picked him up in a fast boat. Transferred him to HMS *Lancaster* and then delivered him to Aruba. He flew in yesterday."

"Excellent."

"I'm curious," Control said. "How did you find him?"

Beatrix had been expecting the question and had given it some thought. "I'll be honest, sir. My first impressions were poor. He was flippant, and I think he might like a drink a little too much. But once we began the operation, he impressed me. He conducted himself well."

"What would you say if I considered him for the Group?"

She thought about that. "I'd say I would want to watch him for a little longer."

"You don't think he has what it takes?"

"No, not that. Just that I'm cautious and there are some things I'd like to be satisfied about before I made him an offer."

"We can talk about that later," Control said, glancing over at Bloom.

Beatrix guessed that he would prefer to keep the

business of the Group between them.

"Yes, sir," she said.

"While we're on the subject of exfiltration," Bloom said, "I believe you were supposed to fly out of Caracas."

"That's right," she said.

"So why didn't you?"

She concentrated on maintaining a professional front. "There was too much heat. The attack at the cache wasn't a coincidence. They knew where we were. And there was a vehicle on its way to Koralev's house while I was there. It didn't feel safe to go through the airport."

Bloom looked down at the file. "So you drove to Guardia, took the ferry to Port of Spain and then flew out of Piarco International?"

"Correct. We have a Group asset in Trinidad. I was able to get a new legend. New passport."

"Indeed," Control said. "Rebecca Smith is no more."

"No, sir. She is officially retired."

The two men shared a look, and Control stood, rapping his knuckles on the surface of the desk.

"Well done, Number One. Good show—a very good show indeed."

Beatrix stood, too.

"Take some time off," he said. "A day or two. Report on Monday. We're working on something new. I'd like you to be involved."

Beatrix nodded and turned away from the desk. She gave a second nod to Bloom, who did not deign to stand, and made her way to the door.

Chapter Fifteen

Control turned towards the window. He could see Vivian Bloom's reflection in the glass: he was still sitting, his right leg folded primly over his left.

"Well?" Control said. "What do you think?"

"She's impressive. Just as you said." Bloom gave a satisfied nod of his head. "Thank you, Control. I appreciate your work on this."

Control ducked his head in acknowledgement. He sat down and drummed his fingers on the desk. "Did you know the Americans had a second team?"

Bloom shook his head. "It wasn't official."

"Off the books?"

"Yes," Bloom said. "The State Department had no idea—still doesn't. My usual contact at the CIA has denied it had anything to do with them."

"So how off the books is 'off the books'?"

"They were protecting the DARPA project. There's a faction growing up around it—we think it involves Manage Risk. It's practically paramilitary."

"They didn't trust us to do the job."

"I don't know that it was that," Bloom said. "More that they felt more comfortable having an insurance policy."

"And happy to wipe out our assets at the same time."

"No witnesses, Control. We might have done the same."

"I'm curious—how did they track them?"

"We believe it was a satellite," Bloom said.

"They re-routed a satellite? Good lord. Manage Risk can do that?"

Bloom spread his hands wide.

"How much would that have cost?" Control said. "They were *that* keen to get him back."

"Indeed. Very keen. You can rest assured that I'm looking into it. I doubt we'll need to involve the Group again, but I'd like to have you on standby."

"Of course," Control said.

Bloom unfolded his legs and stood, wincing with the effort of straightening out his old joints.

"We're both getting old," Control observed.

Bloom smiled, noticing that Control had recognised his discomfort. "I always thought that I would have been retired by now. Should've been."

"How many did the Americans lose?"

"Three. One killed, two shot."

"I told you she was good."

"You did."

"And Koralev? You said they wanted him alive."

"I don't think they really cared. Dead or alive—they just didn't want him in play. All's well that ends well, as far as they're concerned. They're happy with the outcome and we get a gold star we can cash in the next time we need a favour." Bloom stood. "Thanks again."

Control watched him go. He knew that there was a lot that he hadn't been told. It wasn't unusual. He was often given partial information, the motive behind an operation obscured or hidden behind a veil of national security or internecine departmental rivalry. He preferred to have the full picture, but he was experienced enough to know that that was not always going to be possible. Still, he thought, as he turned back to his window and gazed out onto the river, there were depths here that went beyond what was normal. Bloom was holding a lot back. Control wondered if he would ever find out more.

He put it out of mind and picked up the file that Tanner had left on his desk. It was an appraisal. The name on the front of the file was MILTON, MAJOR JOHN, and the sheaf of papers inside was a centimetre thick. He had commissioned the report two weeks ago. Beatrix's approval was encouraging, even if it was equivocal. She was a hard woman to please.

He took his pipe from his pocket, sat down in his chair, and started to read.

Chapter Sixteen

Beatrix took a taxi to Paddington and then caught the Heathrow Express to the airport. She went to the British Airways desk and bought a ticket to Paris with a credit card in the name of Francine Zimmer, the third legend that she had used in the past week. She checked in, the staff photo card in her purse announcing that she was an executive for an advertising agency with clients across Europe. She bought lunch in the airside concession, bought a novel from WHSmith, and waited to board her flight.

#

The flight was uneventful. Beatrix passed through immigration without issue, then went to the train station and bought a Paris metro carnet. She took the train into the city, emerged at Châtelet and crossed the Seine. She descended into St Michel and took the southbound train to Porte d'Orléans. She was vigilant throughout, not expecting to be tailed but drilled to be aware of the possibility, her vigilance given extra edge by the knowledge that to be discovered in Paris now would be fatal for her career. The train pulled into Denfert-Rochereau station. Beatrix waited until the doors started to close before she leapt out of her seat. She pressed them open just enough to squeeze through onto the platform and looked back into the carriage as the train slid into the tunnel. A few people gazed at her, no doubt wondering about her sudden urgency, but there was nothing that might have indicated a frustrated tail. She crossed the platform and waited for a train to take her in the opposite direction.

She was as confident as she could be that she was not being followed. She felt comfortable enough that it was safe to make her way to her destination.

#

The apartment was in the Marais, within walking distance of the Place des Vosges, the Picasso Museum and the Opera Bastille. It had been built in the early 1800s and was located in a quiet, secluded courtyard with trees and plants, paved with period cobblestones. Beatrix unlocked the door and climbed to the second of the four floors. She unlocked the door and paused on the threshold. The place was owned by an interior designer who made a little extra cash by letting it on the side. There were small and intimate rooms, each with wooden shutters and an oak floor. Large windows overlooked the courtyard, and the furniture was a charming hodgepodge of eighteenth-century pieces supplemented by flat-pack items from Ikea and Habitat.

Beatrix gathered herself. She was nervous.

Lucas must have heard the door. He eased silently out of the bedroom, put his finger to his lips and came over to embrace her. She kissed him and pressed herself into his arms. Lucas had no idea what she did for employment; the idea of his ever finding out was anathema to her. He was a good man, and she couldn't predict how he would react if he knew the truth. She had been a soldier before, and that hadn't fazed him, but she operated in a world of grey now, when it had been black and white before. She wasn't prepared to take the risk, even if her silence—and often her dishonesty—was a heavy price to pay.

He trusted her. He had flown to Paris two days ago, taking a sudden leave of absence so he could care for an ailing relative. They had two weeks. That would be a safe enough margin to leave before he returned to London.

His trust ran deeper than leaving the country because of an unexplained phone call from the other side of the world.

She disengaged herself and crossed the room to the open doorway. The bedroom was beyond. It was as charming as the rest of the apartment: a large double bed with a handmade quilt, a vintage rug on the floor, art on the walls—Rothko prints—and a dim lamp in one corner.

Beatrix stepped into the room. There was a crib next to the bed. Lucas had had it delivered from Printemps du Louvre and he had chosen well. It was wooden, painted white and with oblique legs that were reminiscent of vintage design and looked in keeping with the apartment's decor. The baby was wrapped in a swaddle, a tight bundle that enclosed her arms and legs. She was sleeping, her soft breathing the only thing that Beatrix could hear.

She stared at the child, almost unaware of the hand on her shoulder. Lucas was next to her.

She had been thinking about the child ever since she had handed her over to Lucas when they had met at the apartment. She was the reason that she had left Venezuela through Trinidad. She couldn't risk taking her through the airport, and, more to the point, she needed a passport for her. The only risk that she had taken was to ask the Group's stringer in Port of Spain to provide her with two new passports: one for her and one for the child, together with a birth certificate and the associated documentation that would prove that she was Beatrix's child.

The man had asked whether she had a name in mind. She didn't know the name of the child, but Koralev had mentioned Phoenix. Was that her name, or the name of the program that Koralev had been involved with? There was no way of knowing. Beatrix had found her thoughts drifting to her grandmother, a steady presence through a difficult childhood. Her grandmother had been called Isabella—a throwback to the French blood that had always been reputed to run through the family—and the name seemed appropriate.

When the stringer had finished preparing the passports, Beatrix had taken them, turned to the child's and flipped through to the picture page at the end. She had taken the photograph herself, the baby gazing solemnly into the lens of the digital camera that the man had had in his workshop. The details recorded her as a British citizen, noted her date of birth as nine months previous, and noted her name along the bottom.

Rose, Isabella.

It was as good as any.

GET EXCLUSIVE JOHN MILTON MATERIAL

Building a relationship with my readers is the very best thing about writing. I occasionally send newsletters with details on new releases, special offers and other bits of news relating to the John Milton, Beatrix and Isabella Rose and Soho Noir series.

And if you sign up to the mailing list I'll send you this free Milton content:

1. A free copy of the John Milton novella, Tarantula.

2. A copy of the highly classified background check on John Milton before he was admitted to Group 15. Exclusive to my mailing list – you can't get this anywhere else.

You can get the novella and the background check **for free**, by signing up at http://eepurl.com/b1T_NT

IF YOU ENJOYED THIS BOOK…

Reviews are the most powerful tools in my arsenal when it comes getting attention for my books. Much as I'd like to, I don't have the financial muscle of a New York publisher. I can't take out full page ads in the newspaper or put posters on the subway.

(Not yet, anyway).

But I do have something much more powerful and effective than that, and it's something that those publishers would kill to get their hands on.

A committed and loyal bunch of readers.

Honest reviews of my books help bring them to the attention of other readers.

If you've enjoyed this book I would be very grateful if you could spend just five minutes leaving a review (it can be as short as you like) on the book's page.

Thank you very much.

ACKNOWLEDGEMENTS

Thanks to the members of Team Milton for technical advice and support. Thanks to Pauline Nolet and Jennifer McIntyre for editorial assistance. And thanks to you for investing your time in reading this story. I hope you enjoyed it as much as I enjoyed writing it.

ABOUT THE AUTHOR

Mark Dawson is the author of the breakout John Milton, Beatrix Rose and Soho Noir series. He makes his online home at www.markjdawson.com. You can connect with Mark on Twitter at @pbackwriter, on Facebook at www.facebook.com/markdawsonauthor and you should send him an email at mark@markjdawson.com if the mood strikes you.

ALSO BY MARK DAWSON

Have you read them all?

<u>In the Soho Noir Series</u>

Gaslight

When Harry and his brother Frank are blackmailed into paying off a local hood they decide to take care of the problem themselves. But when all of London's underworld is in thrall to the man's boss, was their plan audacious or the most foolish thing that they could possibly have done?

The Black Mile

London, 1940: the Luftwaffe blitzes London every night for fifty-seven nights. Houses, shops and entire streets are wiped from the map. The underworld is in flux: the Italian criminals who dominated the West End have been interned and now their rivals are fighting to replace them. Meanwhile, hidden in the shadows, the Black-Out Ripper sharpens his knife and sets to his grisly work.

The Imposter

War hero Edward Fabian finds himself drawn into a criminal family's web of vice and soon he is an accomplice to their scheming. But he's not the man they think he is - he's far more dangerous than they could possibly imagine.

In the John Milton Series

One Thousand Yards

In this dip into his case files, John Milton is sent into North Korea. With nothing but a sniper rifle, bad intentions and a very particular target, will Milton be able to take on the secret police of the most dangerous failed state on the planet?

Tarantula

In this further dip into his files, Milton is sent to Italy. A colleague who was investigating a particularly violent Mafiosi has disappeared. Will Milton be able to get to the bottom of the mystery, or will he be the next to fall victim to Tarantula?

The Cleaner

Sharon Warriner is a single mother in the East End of London, fearful that she's lost her young son to a life in the gangs. After John Milton saves her life, he promises to help. But the gang, and the charismatic rapper who leads it, is not about to cooperate with him.

Saint Death

John Milton has been off the grid for six months. He surfaces in Ciudad Juárez, Mexico, and immediately finds himself drawn into a vicious battle with the narco-gangs that control the borderlands.

The Driver

When a girl he drives to a party goes missing, John Milton is worried. Especially when two dead bodies are discovered and the police start treating him as their prime suspect.

Ghosts

John Milton is blackmailed into finding his predecessor as Number One. But she's a ghost, too, and just as dangerous as him. He finds himself in de ep trouble, playing the Russians against the British in a desperate attempt to save the life of his oldest friend.

The Sword of God

On the run from his own demons, John Milton treks through the Michigan wilderness into the town of Truth. He's not looking for trouble, but trouble's looking for him. He finds himself up against a small-town cop who has no idea with whom he is dealing, and no idea how dangerous he is.

Salvation Row

Milton finds himself in New Orleans, returning a favour that saved his life during Katrina. When a lethal adversary from his past takes an interest in his business, there's going to be hell to pay.

Headhunters

Milton barely escaped from Avi Bachman with his life. But when the Mossad's most dangerous renegade agent breaks out of a maximum security prison, their second fight will be to the finish.

The Ninth Step

Milton's attempted good deed becomes a quest to unveil corruption at the highest levels of government and murder at the dark heart of the criminal underworld. Milton is pulled back into the game, and that's going to have serious consequences for everyone who crosses his path.

In the Beatrix Rose Series

In Cold Blood

Beatrix Rose was the most dangerous assassin in an off-the-books government kill squad until her former boss betrayed her. A decade later, she emerges from the Hong Kong underworld with payback on her mind. They gunned down her husband and kidnapped her daughter, and now the debt needs to be repaid. It's a blood feud she didn't start but she is going to finish.

Blood Moon Rising

There were six names on Beatrix's Death List and now there are four. She's going to account for the others, one by one, even if it kills her. She has returned from Somalia with another target in her sights. Bryan Duffy is in Iraq, surrounded by mercenaries, with no easy way to get to him and no easy way to get out. And Beatrix has other issues that need to be addressed. Will Duffy prove to be one kill too far?

Blood and Roses

Beatrix Rose has worked her way through her Kill List. Four are dead, just two are left. But now her foes know she has them in her sights and the hunter has become the hunted.

Hong Kong Stories, Vol. 1

Beatrix Rose flees to Hong Kong after the murder of her husband and the kidnapping of her child. She needs money. The local triads have it. What could possibly go wrong?

In the Isabella Rose Series

The Angel

Isabella Rose is recruited by British intelligence after a terrorist attack on Westminster.

Standalone Novels

The Art of Falling Apart

A story of greed, duplicity and death in the flamboyant, super-ego world of rock and roll. Dystopia have rocketed up the charts in Europe, so now it's time to crack America. The opening concert in Las Vegas is a sell-out success, but secret envy and open animosity have begun to tear the group apart.

Subpoena Colada

Daniel Tate looks like he has it all. A lucrative job as a lawyer and a host of famous names who want him to work for them. But his girlfriend has deserted him for an American film star and his main client has just been implicated in a sensational murder. Can he hold it all together?

Printed in Great Britain
by Amazon